The Travel Adventures of PJ Mouse

• in Queensland •

GWYNETH JANE PAGE

Illustrated by Megan Elizabeth

This book is dedicated to my mom
with thanks for all her love and support.

I would like to thank my family for their support and encouragement as I learn to navigate being an independent author. I would also like to express my gratitude to the teacher-librarians of Victoria, B.C.'s elementary schools for their enthusiastic endorsement of my first book, *The Travel Adventures of PJ Mouse – In Canada.*

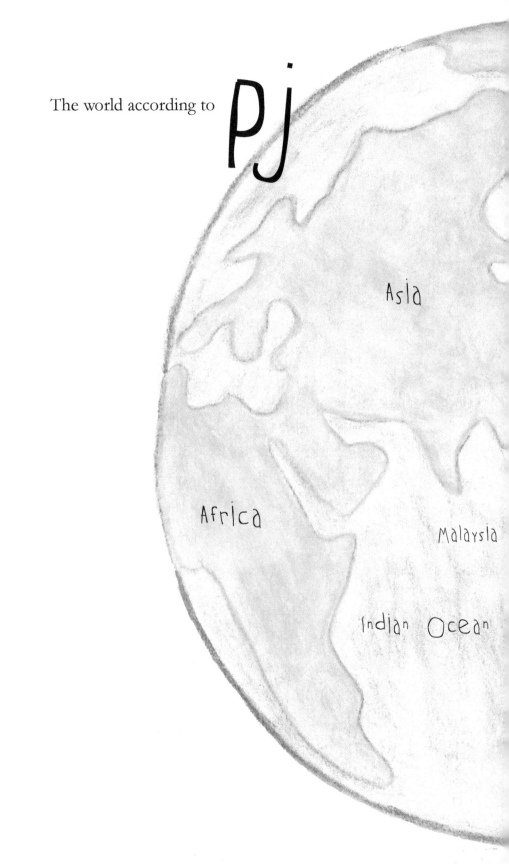

The world according to Pj

Asia

Africa

Malaysia

Indian Ocean

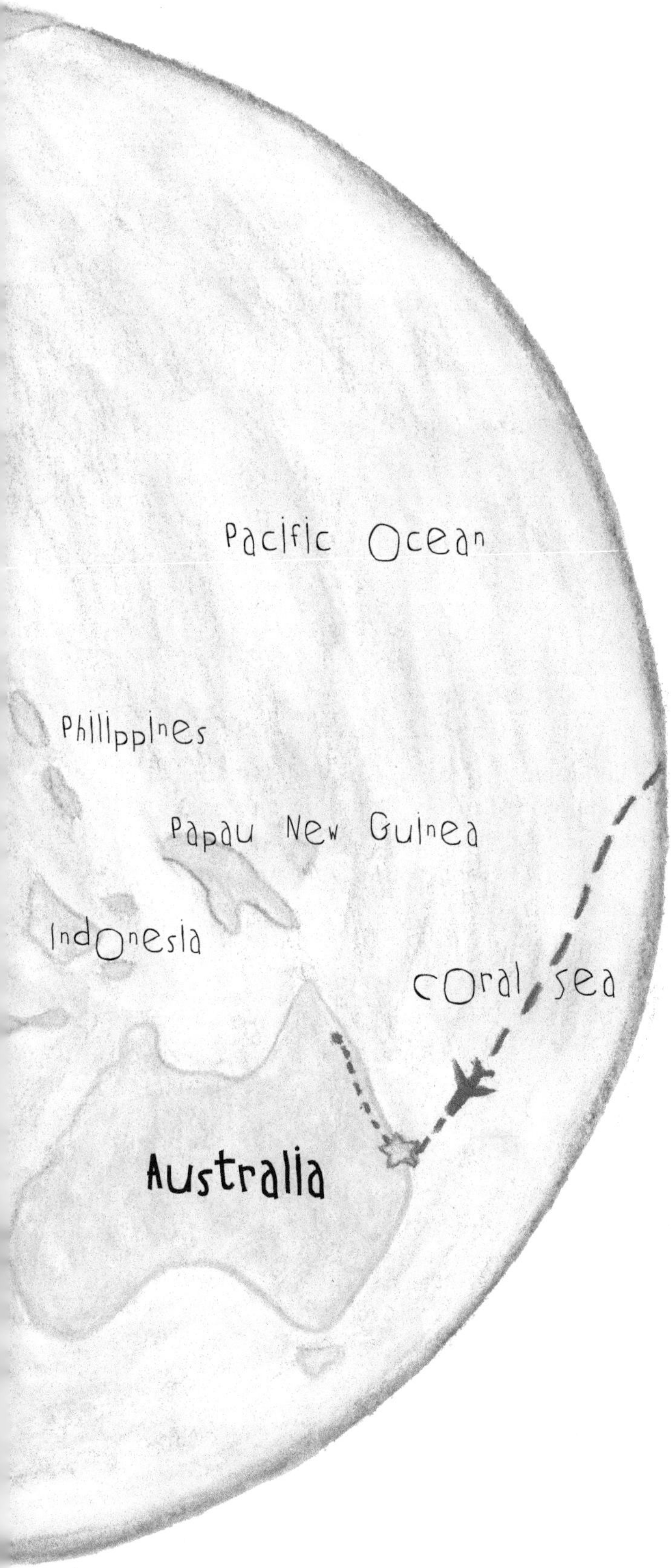

Pacific Ocean

Phillippines

Papau New Guinea

Indonesia

Coral Sea

Australia

Printed in Canada ♻ on recycled paper

FIRST CHOICE BOOKS

firstchoicebooks.ca
Victoria, BC

10 9 8 7 6 5 4 3 2

Table of contents

1   **Chapter One**
In Which PJ Takes a Flight

6   **Chapter Two**
In Which PJ Rides the Tower of Terror and Other Things

12   **Chapter Three**
In Which PJ Goes Boogie Boarding

16   **Chapter Four**
In Which PJ Discovers the Great Barrier Reef

22   **Chapter Five**
In Which PJ Explores the Rainforest and Meets a Lorikeet

28   **Chapter Six**
In Which PJ Encounters Mrs. Turkin

33   **Chapter Seven**
In Which PJ Goes 4 x 4-ing

38   **Chapter Eight**
In Which PJ has a Chat with the Cat

48   **About the Author and Illustrator**

Chapter One

IN WHICH PJ TAKES A FLIGHT

They were going on a big airplane, a really big airplane, to Queensland, which is in a country called Australia. At least, that's what PJ had been told.

PJ felt very special and important with his own suitcase, even if it was a very small suitcase. Just big enough to carry his hat, sunglasses, vest and flip flops—AND he had his very own passport with his picture in it. It was quite a good picture too. Even his ears weren't TOO flopped down in the photo. Yes, he was quite happy about his passport.

At the airport, when they came to the customs inspection, the lady looked at him, looked at his passport, and gave it a big stamp of approval. *She must have liked my photo too,* thought PJ happily.

Then they were walking and walking and walking, down long corridors, past glass rooms with airplanes parked outside of them. At Gate 49 they stopped, and there was their plane. *Oh my goodness, that is an extraordinarily large plane! It must weigh an awful lot! How can something so enormous fly and actually stay up in the air?* thought PJ nervously, until he was distracted by a funny sight on the tail of the plane.

"Why do they have such a funny looking mouse painted on the end of the plane? Its ears are way too small and its tail too big and it seems to be completely lacking in whiskers."

"That's not a mouse. It's a kangaroo," said Rebecca.

"What is a kanga, a roo…what you said?" asked PJ.

"A kangaroo is a kangaroo," stated Megan. "That's just what it is. Just like you are PJ the mouse."

"You are sure it's not a big, funny looking mouse? I mean maybe mouses grow differently in Australia because of being upside down. MAYBE being upside down causes the feet and tail to grow MORE and the ears LESS. So it IS a funny looking mouse and they have just made the mistake of CALLING it a k.a.n.g.a.r.o.o. Which is a very peculiar word by the way and I don't know why anyone would call anything a kangaroo!" declared PJ.

"Well, it's not a mouse. It is a kangaroo. It is a large animal that ONLY lives in Australia and it hops everywhere using its very large feet and tail and it carries its young in a pouch. Even the smaller wallabies are much bigger than you," said Rebecca knowingly.

"OH! Yes well, most things seem to be bigger than me! Wallabies, did you say? What are wallabies? Oh, nevermind!

I don't think I'm going to understand half of what is said to me if they keep coming up with all these funny words," said PJ despairingly. "I still think it looks like a funny kind of mouse!" he muttered.

"Come on. It's time to find our seats," said Mom as they walked down the aisle looking for the letters and numbers that were print-ed on their tickets.

PJ was getting excited at the thought of his first plane ride. Apparently, they gave you yummy food, showed lots of good movies, and there was plenty of room for a small mouse, such as himself.

"Oh look PJ, we're moving!" said Emily excitedly.

Then they were going faster and faster and faster and PJ could feel his stuffing shift to his back.

"We're up in the air! We're flying," said Emily.

"I LOVE TAKING OFF!"

"Me too!" said PJ, "but I think I'll be a different mouse when we land."

"Why on earth would you be different?"

"Well, won't we be on the bottom side of the world, so I'll have to walk on my hands to be right side up? And, well you see, my arms are very small and I don't think I can get them above my head to walk on, and—oh fiddlesticks; it does seem so very troublesome—AND I'm getting a nasty case of stuff-a-lumps in my back, which causes me to be very unbalanced," declared PJ miserably.

"Silly mouse. You do worry over the funniest things. You'll still be able to use your legs to walk and still be right side up," Emily replied.

"But how can that be? If I draw a picture of me standing on the bottom of the world I am always upside down!" PJ declared.

"Hmmm. You do have a point. But I suppose the world is just a ball in space really and has no sides. No particular part is up or down. Do you see?"

"No, I can't say that I do. Every globe that I have ever seen shows Australia on the bottom. Don't they call it 'the land down under'?"

"Well, yes. But, I am positive everyone still walks on their feet and NOT on their hands. Now let's see you. Oh, you do look a bit lumpy," said Emily as she shook PJ back into shape.

"Oh, thank you. No more stuff-a-lumps. Ahhhhhhhhh," said PJ with relief, as he settled back in his chair to watch the first movie.

Many, many hours later, the weary travellers stepped off the plane at the Brisbane airport.

"The wonders of the modern age!" exclaimed Dad. "After a few hours of riding in a cylindrical bus, you leave the grey, gloom and rain of winter…

…and you arrive into the sunny blue skies of summer."

"What are we going to do first Daddy?" asked Emily.

"Well, tomorrow we could go to Dreamworld. It's a big theme park with lots of fun rides."

"Oh dear, and just when I had got rid of my stuff-a-lumps," said PJ.

"Funny little mouse," said Emily affectionately.

chapter Two

IN WHICH PJ RIDES THE TOWER OF TERROR AND OTHER THINGS

Emily was bouncing up and down in excitement. She wanted to go on the Motocoaster ride first. She had never been on a motorcycle before, and was not sure if she really fancied getting on a real one, so the thought of driving her own motorcycle on a ride was very thrilling.

They lined up for the Motocoaster and when it was their turn, Emily climbed onto the big yellow motorcycle and PJ clambered into the sidecar that was attached to her bike. The automatic harness came down and strapped them in. Then the traffic lights went from RED to YELLOW to GREEN and they were launched from the starting gate at a great speed. The motorcycle went screaming around the bends and up and down the hills, the wind was in their faces and they started to laugh with the thrill of the ride. Then the ride slowed and it was over as suddenly as it had begun.

"That was so much fun! Can we go on that again?" asked PJ.

"PJ, you must be getting more brave. Weren't you scared?" asked Emily

"Oh, you're right. No, I don't think I was. I was having too much fun to be scared. That's so unlike me. How delightful," replied PJ happily.

"I think we should go on the Wipe-Out next," said Peter, "it's a surfing ride and we have to try surfing when in Australia."

This time they went upside-down, and sideways, and backwards and forwards and…and…and *oh my, which way was up, and was that a REAL shark in the water? They must not be very good at surfing*, thought PJ. *I thought you just stood up on the board on top of the wave.* Then, the ride stopped and they got off. PJ's legs felt just a bit wobbly.

"Did you see the SIZE of the shark that was below us in the water?" asked PJ.

"It was not a REAL shark you know!" said Peter.

"Oh, well that is a relief. But I DO wish you had told me that BEFORE we got on the ride. All the same, my legs are still a bit wobbly. I don't think I am very good at surfing," stated PJ.

"You're not supposed to be good at surfing on that ride. That's the whole point. It IS called the Wipe-Out after all."

"Oh well. In that case, can we go on it again? I would have much less to worry about this time," said PJ happily.

"Next stop...the Tower of Terror," said Rebecca.

Oh my goodness, gracious me, I don't know if I like the sound of that, thought PJ. *I'm a very small mouse and I get scared easily. Oh fiddlesticks, it doesn't look as though my being more brave lasted very long,* thought PJ despairingly.

They had to stand in a long line-up to wait for the ride, which gave PJ plenty of time to think about how scared he was. With a name like the Tower of Terror, it did not sound at all promising.

At the end of the line, they all climbed into a big metal car that was on a track.

"Is this the Tower of Terror?" asked PJ, thinking that it did not seem TOO bad. *It's just a car on a straight track. Although, I'm so small I can't actually see where the track goes, even from the front row. Oh dear.*

"Yes," replied Emily, and then her words were lost somewhere behind them.

Oh goodness gracious me, thought PJ as the air whizzed past his ears. *I do believe I have left my stuffing in the back row of the car. I hope it's still there when we get out.* PJ looked up and saw that Emily's long brown hair was streaming out behind her in a straight line and in front of him was the clear blue sky. *Is the car going to become a rocket?* thought PJ. *Oh fiddlesticks.* Then, Emily's hair was in her face and all over the place and PJ felt like his stuffing was now somewhere off in space. He was quite sure he did not have any anymore. And then they came to a sudden stop. Everyone was laughing. *OH, THAT WAS FUN!*

"How fast was that?" asked Peter, hopping about excitedly.

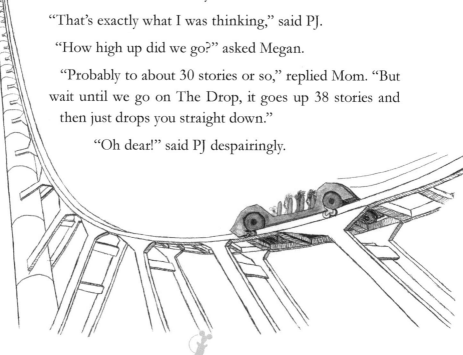

"I read that it goes from 0 to 160 kmh in 3 seconds and pulls 7Gs. I was also told that it doubles the power intake of the entire park to launch the car," said Rebecca.

"OH!" said Peter and Emily in awe.

"That's exactly what I was thinking," said PJ.

"How high up did we go?" asked Megan.

"Probably to about 30 stories or so," replied Mom. "But wait until we go on The Drop, it goes up 38 stories and then just drops you straight down."

"Oh dear!" said PJ despairingly.

They approached a tall, tall tower and, looking up, could barely see the top of the ride.

"Here we go. Sit in the chair and pull the harness over your head and hold on tight to PJ," said Dad.

Yes, please do! Oh my, we are extraordinarily high up in the air. I feel like I can see forever, to the end of the edge of the world. "Have we reached the top?" PJ asked as the ride came to a stop.

"I sure hope so," said Emily in a shaky voice.

"But nothing seems to be happening."

Oh I do hope they have not forgotten us up here.

UH OH...

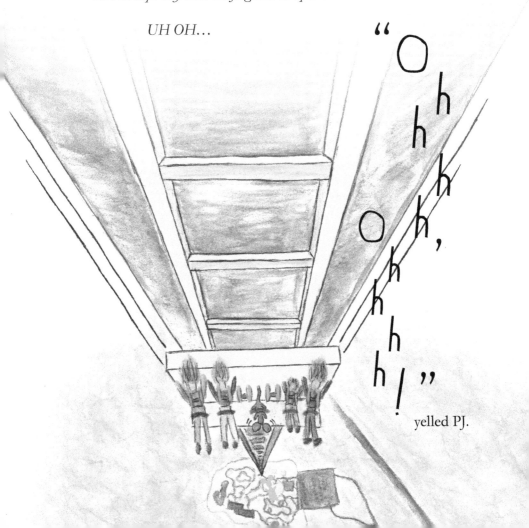

yelled PJ.

My poor stuffing. I will NEVER *find it now. I hope my ears stay on. At least I am sitting on my tail. I think I need to close my eyes.* "Have we stopped again?" asked PJ, without daring to open his eyes.

"Yes," said Emily, "but my tummy still seems to be going."

Oh hurray, I am back on the ground.

"Am I still in one piece, Emily? Are my ears still there? Do I still have all my stuffing? "

"Funny little mouse, of course you do. But that was a bit scary, wasn't it?" said Emily.

"Come on, let's go see the koalas in the petting zoo. Maybe PJ can find a baby koala that's just his size," said Megan as she ruffled Emily's hair. "Look at your hair Emily, it looks like you have not brushed it in years."

PJ and Emily looked at Mom, Dad, Rebecca, Megan and Peter, and then laughed. They did look a bit wild.

Maybe tomorrow they could do something a little more tame, like surfing or boogie-boarding at the beach.

Chapter Three

IN WHICH PJ GOES BOOGIE BOARDING

It was a warm, sunny day on the Gold Coast. The sand at Burleigh Beach was white, the ocean blue, and PJ felt quite relaxed lazing under the beach umbrella in the shade.

"What are you thinking about PJ?" asked Peter.

"Thinking? Hmmm, I don't think I was thinking anything at all. My head seems to be full of stuffing today."

"It is a very relaxing kind of a day," said Emily.

"Yes. That's just it. I was thinking relaxing thoughts. Must have worked, as I seem to have relaxed myself out of any thoughts at all."

"I was thinking about going boogie-boarding," said Peter. "Anyone want to join me?"

"It does look like lots of fun," said PJ drowsily.

"Well, I'm ready for some excitement. Come on, Emily, grab PJ and let's go."

And with that, PJ found himself whisked away.

Emily and Peter picked up their boogie-boards, which looked kind of like half size surfboards, and headed for the waves.

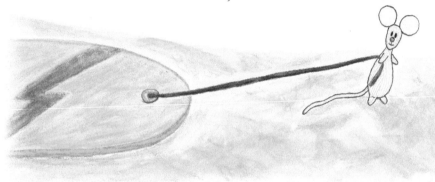

"Wow, it's so warm!" said Emily.

"I believe you," said PJ nervously from his perch on Emily's shoulder.

"Really, it feels like a bath."

"Yes, that may be, but it does not LOOK like a bath. Baths generally DON'T have very big WAVES in them."

"They're not that big. See, I am still standing," said Emily.

"You are?! Oh, so you are. I can see your feet."

"Come on. You sit on the front of the board and when the next wave comes I'll push off and we'll ride to shore."

So, PJ perched himself at the front of the board and suddenly found himself zooming along on top of the wave. He could see the white, frothy crest of the big wave just below his feet. *Hmmmm, maybe mouses shouldn't look down when boogie-boarding*, he thought, and looked up.

"Phhhttt," said PJ as he wiped the salt spray out of his mouth and eyes. *Hmmmm, maybe looking sideways would be better,* and turned his head. *Ahhhhhh, that is definitely much preferable. Oh my, but we are zipping along at quite a rate.*

This IS fun after all!

wheeeeee! "This is soooooo exciting!" cried PJ, as they rushed towards the shore.

"Yippeeee! Wheeeee! This is so much fun!" said Peter and Emily, in unison, as they neared the shore—and PJ went hurtling head over heels across the beach.

Oh fiddlesticks. That was an abrupt end, thought PJ, as he landed with a face-plant into the beach. "Ppphhhhhtt! Oh, hello," said PJ, as he lifted his face out of the sand at Megan's feet.

"You funny little mouse. That was quite a performance. I didn't know you could do cartwheels."

"No, I didn't either. But, well, I did just have lots of practice."

"Are you ok?"

"I think so," said PJ, spitting out another mouthful of sand. Getting up, he shook himself off. "But I think I might have become a part of the beach or maybe the beach became a part of me, I'm not quite sure which."

"You are quite a sight. Come on. I'll take you back to Emily and this time lie down and hold on to the strap."

"That sounds very sensible. Why didn't I think of that? My head must be stuffed with cotton or something. My relaxing thoughts from earlier have chased all the practical ones completely away. But then, now I think of it, I hardly ever seem to have sensible thoughts like that."

"Funny little mouse, come on."

This time PJ laid himself down, held onto the strap, and they rode into shore without mishap. Peter, Emily and PJ had so much fun. They caught wave after wave until they were all quite exhausted—and very sandy and wet.

chapter Four

IN WHICH PJ DISCOVERS THE
GREAT BARRIER REEF

Oh, I do hope the fish will be friendly, thought PJ, as he donned his snorkel and mask.

"Are you all ready Emily?" asked Emily's mom.

"I think so, but do the fish bite, Mommy?"

"No sweetie, but they might nibble your toes."

"PJ's toes are very small, I hope they don't nibble too much."

Oh dear, me too! thought PJ.

...And into the clear, turquoise-blue water they went.

16

What fun. The fish are friendly, thought PJ with relief, *and they're all coming to say hello.* At least he hoped they were, but he did not quite fully understand 'Fish'.

"Hello," said PJ.

"Why g'day, little fellow. I say, I have never met a fish quite like you before. Why, where are your fins, and that is a very strange snout you have there," said a big, yellow, polka-dotted fish.

"I am a mouse and this is not my snout—it's a snorkel. It helps me breathe under water."

"Fascinating. So, you mean to tell me that you can't breathe under water. I reckon that is most unfortunate."

"Yes, certainly. But, you see, I can breathe when on land. I have a very cute little nose underneath this snorkel and mask and it is quite adequate most of the time."

"You are very adaptable. Congratulations!"

"Congratulations for what?"

"For being able to breathe in the water AND on land. Very clever indeed."

"OH. Yes, well, thank you very much," said PJ, not really understanding why he would be considered clever since he was not the actual inventor of the snorkel and mask.

"It was lovely to meet you but I must be on my way." And, with that, the large fish swam off into the distance.

PJ carried on with exploring the reef. It was incredible! Beautiful! PJ had had no idea that there were so many colourful fish in the ocean, and such a variety of coral. Some of the coral seemed to be waving at him, some seemed to just be little critters with eyes looking at him and some blew bubbles. There was pink, purple, yellow and blue. Some coral looked like feathers, or tails. *I think that is an enormous clam*, he thought, *with purple lips*. It was all so fascinating. In the reef were thousands of fish. They were all different sizes and shapes. There were huge funny looking fish that were almost ugly. Then there were small beautiful fish with lots of colours and spots or stripes, or zig zag patterns.

*I wonder if I swim with the fish, they will think
I'm a fish too?* he thought. *But I suppose
I might not be quite colourful enough, as
well as having a funny snout. They would
have to think Emily is a fish though as her
bathing suit is VERY bright. Oh dear,
dear me—where IS Emily?*

PJ bobbed to
the surface. Emily
and her mom were
just little specks off in the distance.

"Oh, HELP!" *I do seem to be moving
very, very quickly for a small mouse.*

"G'day, can I be of service?" enquired Mr.
Turkin, the local loggerhead turtle, as he poked his
head above the water next to PJ.

"Oh, hello. Yes, please, if you would be so kind. I seem to have
drifted off. I am quite far from shore, at least further than I would
really LIKE to be," said PJ.

"Ah yes! I reckon that would be the rip."

"Pardon?"

"The rip-tide. It is a very strong current and it has caught you
and is taking you out to sea," said the turtle in a tone of voice that
was a little too calm and matter of fact for PJ's liking.

"Oh fiddlesticks. I really don't WANT to go out to sea. Do you
know, might there be ANY other options BESIDES the one of
going out to sea?" enquired PJ.

"But of course. If you put one arm up and hold it up, then a
lifeguard will come to your rescue."

"That might work for someone who has regular length arms, but you see, mine are very small, AND they are blue and white and so match the colour of the water quite well. I am not at all sure that a lifeguard WOULD be able to see my arms."

"Hmmm, yes, well, in that case, it might just be best if you hop on my back and I will deliver you ashore."

"That sounds MUCH nicer than being swept out to sea. But why doesn't the rip take you out to sea?" asked PJ

"I am familiar with these waters and a very strong swimmer. I swim thousands of miles through the oceans."

"Thousands of miles—that is a very long swim, isn't it?"

"Yes, it is. But, I have lots of mates to visit along the way. Come on then. Hop on and off we go. Can't dilly-dally all day. I've got places to go and mates to see," said Mr. Turkin.

Back at the beach a very worried Emily was scanning the ocean for her lost little mouse when she saw a huge turtle coming her way. "Look, Mommy, look! It's an enormous turtle and I think I see PJ on his back."

Mr. Turkin waded very slowly up onto the beach to deliver the soggy, sad PJ back to Emily. She picked PJ up, gave him a squeeze, dripping water everywhere, and then gave Mr. Turkin a pat of gratitude for saving her beloved mouse.

"Thank you, Mr. Turkin," said PJ.

"No worries, mate," replied the helpful turtle, and off he swam.

"You silly little mouse, why did you wander off?"

"I wanted to swim with the fish. There are so many of them and they are all so pretty. They were orange, red, blue and green, yellow and purple, and they had spots and stripes, and, and, and they were VERY friendly. But it sure does tickle when they nibble your toes."

"Funny little mouse."

"Come on, you two. It's time for a picnic on the beach and for PJ to dry off a bit in the sunshine."

"Can we snorkel more after lunch, mommy?"

"Of course, but this time, I will tie PJ to you with a shoestring."

Chapter Five

IN WHICH PJ EXPLORES THE RAINFOREST AND MEETS A LORIKEET

PJ and the family had taken a twenty minute car ride inland from the Gold Coast to explore Mt. Tamborine. It was a steep ride up the mountain, but once they reached the top, it was totally flat. There were quaint little houses, cafes, vineyards, cheese shops, and art studios.

The tropical plants in the area were prolific and fragrant. The 'yesterday, today and tomorrow' plant had dark purple, light purple and white flowers on it and smelled like a little bit of heaven. The jacaranda trees were like huge umbrellas of purple flowers and the poinsettia trees looked like huge red umbrellas.

They decided to take a stroll in the rainforest. The palm trees and the strangler fig trees went way up to the sky. The sunlight filtered through the green canopy far, far above PJ's head. PJ felt extremely small, even smaller than normal.

Some of the birds were quite loud. He could hear the kookaburras. *The noise they make really does sound like someone laughing. And it is very contagious*, thought PJ, as he started to laugh himself, until an ibis went by and startled him. The ibis were not loud. They were very silent, but you sure could SMELL them! *YUCK! I think I will keep my distance from them, I don't want to get stepped on,* he thought. He watched the tall birds walk around on their skinny legs, as they scavenged for food with their long, curved beaks.

Then there were the lorikeets. They especially seemed to like to chatter with each other. Even though he could hear them he found it very difficult to find the colourful birds in the green trees.

I wonder if I climb one of these twisty fig trees if I could join in the lorikeet conversation, thought PJ.

So he started to climb the tree, following its twisty trunk up and up and up and up and up until he looked down and—

"Oh dear, oh my, oh help!" said PJ. "Oh HELP, oh dear, oh my!" he said again a bit louder.

"G'day," said a voice from a nearby branch.

PJ looked around. He thought he had heard someone, but he could not see anyone in the branches of the fig tree.

"Hello," he said timidly.

"G'day. Who might you be? You don't look like any bird I've ever seen before," said the voice.

"Hello. Who's that?"

"I'm here in the leaves. Can you see me now?" asked the lorikeet, hopping into a spot of sunshine.

"Oh hello. Oh my, yes, I most certainly CAN see you now. I really do not know how I can NOT have seen you before. Why, you look like a rainbow, a very, very bright rainbow. My name is PJ and I am not a bird of any sort, I am a small mouse of only TWO colours."

"G'day. Mr. Keets, a bird of many colours, at your service. Don't little mouses of only two colours belong on the ground, mate?"

"Well, yes. That seems like a much better idea now. I am frightfully high up and I don't think I like it as much as I THOUGHT I would. I did so want to meet you and join in your conversation. But now I think I would MUCH prefer being back down there—oh dear, dear I can't look— with Peter and Emily."

"Yes, well, I reckon you are right about one thing. You are frightfully high up. Probably about 150 feet or so."

"150 feet—oh my. That would be about 148 feet more than what I am comfortable with. It must have taken an awfully long time for this tree to get to be that tall."

"You're right again, my little mate. This here tree has

been around for going on 1000 years. Quite impressive, wouldn't you say?"

"Well, yes, that is very impressive indeed. AND maybe that explains why I am so little. I have just not lived long enough to be tall. NOT that I would really want to be THIS tall."

"Hmmm. Yes, quite. If you were THIS tall you might be a bit frightening. Certainly nobody would think of you as a cute LITTLE mouse."

"You do have a point," agreed PJ, "but, I still have no idea how I am to get down from this extremely tall tree. I don't suppose there would be an ELEVATOR hidden in the middle of the tree, would there?" PJ questioned hopefully.

"No, I shouldn't think so. No elevator that I am aware of. But, I reckon if you climb onto my back and hold on good and tight I could fly you down to join your mates," offered Mr. Keets.

"I would be ever so grateful if you could. I did wonder what it's like to be a bird. It would be a wonderful adventure," said PJ as he climbed onto the lorikeets bright green back.

Meanwhile, Peter and Emily were looking for PJ, who seemed to have very suddenly gone missing.

"I can't see him anywhere, Emily. He was just on your shoulder and then he wasn't. He is such a little mouse, he could be quite hard to see in amongst all these palm fronds."

"But he can't just disappear. He's small but not invisible. You don't suppose he went up a tree do you, so that he could see better?" asked Emily as she gazed up into the foliage far above her head.

"I see him. Look there. That lorikeet is chatting to him, see, on that branch," said Peter. "Oh, lucky little mouse. Looks like he is going to have a mouse's version of a helicopter tour above the rainforest."

PJ was holding on tightly as they took off above the dense foliage of the rainforest canopy. Peter and Emily looked liked little dots far below him. The forest was very green. He could see the tall palm trees in between the immense strangler figs and there was a lovely little stream running through it. There were a multitude of different coloured birds calling out to each other from their hiding spots amongst the branches. *Being a bird is really quite fun*, thought PJ.

At last Mr. Keets landed on top of Peter's head. "I do say, what a nice landing spot. Very soft indeed." Mr. Keets leaned over, peered into young Peter's eyes…

…and almost pitched poor little PJ onto the ground at Peter's feet. "I say, thank you for being so obliging and allowing me to land on your head. Sorry little mouse, you are so light I quite forgot I had a passenger."

"Thank you very much for the ride Mr. Keets. That was ever such an exciting adventure. It was fun to be a bird for a while, but I do think in the end, that I am quite content being a little mouse on the ground."

"Thank you, Mr. Keets, for helping PJ," said Emily, who was very happy to have PJ returned to her.

"No worries, young miss—glad to be of service. Mind if I ride along for a while, see what it is like to only look at things from the ground?" asked the lorikeet as he hopped about on Peter's head.

"Not at all," said Peter.

They all set off together to explore the rest of the rainforest.

chapter six

IN WHICH PJ ENCOUNTERS MRS. TURKIN

They were at Mon Repos in Bundaberg. They were waiting for the park ranger to come and take them to the protected beach where the loggerhead turtles came at night to lay their eggs. PJ had on his badge. It had a big #2 on it, which meant he was part of group two and would get to see the second turtle of the night that came onto the beach. PJ knew it was a number two because he had learned to count that high.

"How long will we have to wait?" asked PJ.

"Hopefully not too long since we are in group two," replied Megan as she gazed out at the moonlit ocean.

"Look there! What's that?" said Peter in a hushed voice, pointing to a rounded shape emerging out of the water.

"Shhhh, don't scare it off," said Mom. "If you startle them when they are emerging from the ocean then they will take fright and not come and lay their eggs."

PJ watched as an enormous turtle slowly lumbered its way up the beach. It came to a stop right beside PJ and, using its flippers, sprayed PJ with a massive amount of sand.

"Ppphhhhttttt!"

"I say, what did you do that for?" asked PJ, shaking himself free of sand.

"OH! So sorry. Didn't see you there. You are awfully small you know. Really, you should not be so small and startle a turtle like that when they are in the midst of a great undertaking."

"What great undertaking might that be?"

"I am going to dig a very large hole."

"In that case, I think I'll move or I'll be buried under a pile of sand. It won't take much of a pile of sand to cover me."

"Yes well, since you are so tiny and I am an extremely large turtle in the process of digging a very, very big hole, I think moving is a grand idea. Try sitting in front of me, out of the line of spray," said the turtle obligingly.

And so the turtle continued to dig, and dig, and dig, and dig, and dig, and dig.

When the hole was very large indeed the turtle took a short rest.

"Are you done now?" asked PJ, thinking that really, watching a turtle dig a hole lost some of its appeal after a very short amount of time.

"I'm done digging the hole," said the turtle in a tired sort of manner. "Now I need to lay my eggs."

"You must lay awfully large eggs if you need such a big hole to put them into."

"No, they're actually very tiny. There are just lots and lots of them."

"Smaller than me? And how many will you have? Will you have more than two? I know how to count to two as I'm smart for a mouse. Two is big for a number, don't you think? I mean, it is twice as big as one."

"Yes, they will be even smaller than you. And I will lay a lot more than two, even more than one hundred."

"But you are so enormous. How is that possible that they can be so small?" asked PJ, focusing on what was important to him and not really grasping the concept of what more than one hundred was.

"My, you do ask a lot of questions for a small mouse. But, even I started out being very little. When I was a baby, I was only two inches long, and now I am four feet."

"Oh. I wonder. Do you think there is any chance I might grow?"

"I shouldn't think so. I would imagine you are a perfectly good size for a mouse. My name is Mrs. Turkin by the way and who might you be?"

"My name is PJ. And I do believe I met your husband. He rescued me from a rip that I got caught in when snorkeling at the Whitsundays."

"Ah. So you're PJ. He mentioned you were a very cute little mouse and, I must say, I do agree. I'm glad to have met you. Now, I must concentrate for I have a lot of eggs to lay."

"I'll be as quiet as a mouse," promised PJ.

A while later, Emily said to her mom, "Look, the turtle is filling the hole with ping-pong balls."

"They do look like ping-pong balls, but those are the eggs," Mom said as Emily and PJ gazed into the hole that Mrs. Turkin was starting to cover over with sand.

"Now what happens? Will the babies be able to get out?" asked Emily.

"Well, the sand is like their nest. And the different temperatures at the top and bottom of the hole determine whether the little turtles are male or female when they hatch out. After a while they all hatch out and run for the ocean. It used to be that only fifty percent of the baby turtles made it to the ocean because wildlife and dogs would pick them off of the beach. Now that they are protected the park rangers try to make sure one hundred percent of the turtles make it to the ocean. Then they swim thousands of miles away and they won't come back here until they need to lay their own eggs," replied Rebecca.

"Wow, that's amazing. Do they all come back here to lay their eggs?" asked Emily.

"Only the females return to the beach of their birth and they still have to avoid being caught by people who like to make them into soup or use their shells as art," said Rebecca.

"Art! Soup! I'm glad nobody wants to make me into art or soup. How horrible," exclaimed PJ. "I hope you and all your babies will be okay Mrs. Turkin."

"Why thank you PJ. I hope so too."

"I would love to watch the babies hatch," said Peter.

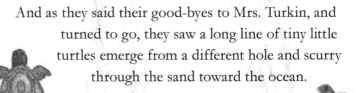

And as they said their good-byes to Mrs. Turkin, and turned to go, they saw a long line of tiny little turtles emerge from a different hole and scurry through the sand toward the ocean.

chapter seven

IN WHICH PJ GOES 4 X 4-ING

They had taken a ferry over to Fraser Island for the purpose of going 4 x 4-ing along the beach. PJ was feeling quite excited as he had never gone 4 x 4-ing before and he thought it would be a great adventure.

"G'day, folks. My name's Mick, and I'll be your bus driver today. If you would all like to climb aboard, we'll get going."

"Come on, PJ. I want to get a window seat so we can see everything," said Emily.

"Look at the size of those tires! Are they bigger than normal or am I shrinking?" asked PJ.

"G'day, little mate. Those are special tires, extra large, for driving on the sand highway," replied Mick.

"Oh, well, I'm glad that they are extra large and I am not shrinking," said PJ with relief.

"Ummm, pardon me, but did you say that the highway was made of sand?" queried Emily.

"That's right little miss. This whole island is made of sand. It's the largest sand island in the world. One hundred and twenty kilometers long and twenty four kilometers wide."

"But how can it be all sand, it has TREES on it?" said PJ, feeling somewhat confused. "Don't trees need DIRT?"

"You ask very smart questions for a little mouse."

"Why, thank you very much," replied PJ, feeling very pleased.

"Fraser Island is very special. The sand has a type of fungi in it that gives the plants the nutrients they need to grow and survive. Now, that's enough of a lesson for the present, I reckon we should go for a ride. Sit down and hold on tight!"

And with that, the bus roared to life and they went speeding down the sand highway. There were quite a few other types of 4 x 4 vehicles on the highway, racing down the long stretch of pure white sand—past all the pic-nickers??

"Look at all those daft people having their picnics in the middle of a designated highway. Who in their right mind takes their family out for a picnic in the middle of a highway?"

"It does seem odd. But then, except for the vehicles racing up and down, it looks like a normal beach. This is super fun to be racing along way up high like this," said Emily. "Where are you taking us to?"

"I am taking you to a lake where you can go for a swim, and then to a very special stream."

"What is so special about the stream?" asked PJ.

"It's a surprise. You will have to tell me if you notice what is different about it when we get there," said Mick mysteriously. "Here we are at the lake. Everyone can pile out and go for a dip to cool off. I hope you all brought your cozzies!"

"Brought our whats?" asked Emily.

"Your cozzies. Your bathing costumes," replied Mick.

"Oh. You mean our swimsuits?"

"That's right, little miss. I reckon we do have a few unique Aussie terms. For instance, university is 'uni,' Christmas is 'Chrissie,' bathing suit is 'cozzie,' popsicles are 'ice blocks,' sunglasses are 'sunnies,' hello is 'g'day,' and friends are 'mates'," said Mick helpfully.

Funny how everywhere I go, there is always something I do not understand, thought PJ, *even if people are speaking English.* Still, the lake was beautiful. PJ felt he could be quite happy staying here forever, even if he didn't understand everything that was said. The sky was blue, the sun and sand were warm, the water cool and refreshing—life was truly idyllic! What more could a small mouse ask for? PJ sighed with contentment.

"Right. Time to head for the stream. Everyone climb aboard please."

Oh fiddlesticks. And just when I was about to have a lovely mouse-nap without the cat using me as a pillow, thought PJ.

Once again they set off racing along the white sands in the 4x4 bus. Eventually they came to a stop and climbed out of the bus. Mick guided them through the tropical forest until he came to an abrupt halt.

"Why did we stop here?" asked Emily.

"This is your surprise," stated Mick.

"But I thought our surprise was something to do with a stream and there is no stream here," replied PJ.

"Ah, but there is!"

"There is?"

"Yep!"

"But I don't SEE a stream and I can't HEAR a stream. Are you sure you're not lost?" asked PJ.

"I reckon I'm in the right spot little mate. Maybe you're just not looking hard enough."

"But I don't usually need to look TOO hard to find a stream, since they make LOTS of noise as they splash around rocks," said Emily. "Are you SURE it is here?"

"Positive!"

"LOOK Emily! I think I found it! The water is totally clear and it doesn't seem to be making any kind of a sound at all," said PJ in amazement.

"Wow! I've never seen a stream like this before. Why is it so silent?"

"It's because there aren't any rocks, so there is nothing for the water to splash against. That is why it is so special. You can't hear it and it is almost invisible because the water is so clear. Now, isn't that a nice surprise?" asked Mick.

"It's very unique. I bet none of our friends back home have ever seen anything like this!" stated PJ. "Thanks, Mick. It has been a great day. I have so many things to tell the cat about when I get home."

"No worries, little mate," replied Mick with a smile. "Do you head home soon?"

"Yes, I think we leave in a couple days," sighed PJ.

"Well, I hope you come back and visit us again sometime."

"That would be so wonderful. I have loved being in Australia. It is so amazing here."

"Happy to have met with your approval, little mate," said Mick, smilingly.

Chapter Eight

IN WHICH PJ HAS A CHAT WITH THE CAT

PJ was having a lovely nap. He was reminiscing about all the fantastic places he had seen on the coast of Queensland, while trying to recover from his jet-lag.

"MEOW!"

"Oh fiddlesticks! Must you always interrupt my mouse-naps?" said PJ indignantly.

"My name is NOT Fiddlesticks. I know I have an extraordinary number of very fine names, but I am pretty sure that Fiddlesticks is not one of them."

"Yes, yes, I know that, Fuzzy Beast. Fiddlesticks is just an expression I use in certain situations—such as when large masses of white fur are intent upon disturbing my sleep and sitting on my stuffing."

"Well, I have missed using you as a pillow. Where have you been? I have been quite desolate with the whole family gone."

"We were in Australia. We had a great time exploring the state of Queensland. It's so beautiful there; amazing beaches, super warm ocean water for things like snorkeling and boogie-boarding, really funny looking wildlife, incredible rainforests. Oh, I could just go on and on, there were so many fun things to do and see."

"Yes, well, if you are going to go on and on, then I'm going to go and find somewhere quieter to sleep. I really am most put out that I have to be left behind all the time. It is most unfair!"

"I'm sorry that you are so disgruntled. But, honestly, I don't think travelling would suit you all that much. For one, you would not be able to sleep eighteen hours a day. Two, you would have to go in a cage on the plane, and the plane ride is very, very long. And three, a lot of the things we did involved water, and you know how much you dislike getting wet."

"Oh, well, if you put it like that, I suppose I'm okay with staying home sleeping and guarding the house. I do dislike water."

"Besides, I did bring you a present," said PJ.

"That might cheer me up a little, or it might not, depends what it is really."

"Here you are," said PJ, pulling out a small package.

"What is that?"

"It's a small, stuffed, toy koala. A type of animal that is only found in Australia."

"And what am I supposed to do with a small, stuffed koala exactly?" asked the cat in a it-still-does-not-make-up-for-leaving-me-at-home tone of voice.

"Well, I had thought you could use him as a cat toy and chase him round the house. I was hoping it might distract you from the thought of chasing small mouses. Or, maybe, you could use him as a pillow as he is cute, and small and stuffed like me, oh, and very, very soft."

"Hmmm, well I will give it some thought. But he does look a little bit too small, and not as well stuffed as you, to make a really good sort of pillow. But thanks anyway. I guess it at least shows that you thought of me while you were off gallivanting around the world."

"Did you do anything at all while we were away?" asked PJ.

"Hmmm. Well, let's see. I guess I did make a new friend. I was looking around the house for a new pillow to replace you and came across this fellow who goes by the name of Star Bear. He resides in Peter's room. Turned out to be quite comfy as far as stuffed pillows go."

"Star Bear. That is an interesting name, almost as good as some of the names you have. What is this Star Bear like exactly?" asked PJ.

"I'll go fetch him and you can judge for yourself," and with that Fuzzy went off in the direction of Peter's room to try and find Star Bear.

Humph. One short trip away and I've already been replaced as a pillow. Mind you it might not be such a bad thing to share the joy of being squished by that mass of fur, thought PJ.

"I'm back, and I found Star Bear. Here he is," said the cat, as he dropped a little white bear, all covered in colourful stars, beside PJ on the bed.

"Ah-ha! Now I see why they call you Star Bear," said PJ.

"Why of course you do. Everyone does. It is because I am a STAR, famous throughout the entire world," replied the bear.

"You ARE? OH! Hmmm, funny, I had never heard of you before just now."

"Really. How very unusual. Quite amazing really! And who exactly might you be?" asked the bear.

"This is PJ Mouse," said the cat. "I usually use him as a pillow, but then he went on holiday and that is when I found you instead."

"PJ Mouse. Well, it is very nice to meet

you, I am sure, even if you haven't ever heard of me before. Are you quite, quite sure about that, as it does seem highly unlikely. I mean I am a STAR Bear after all."

"Yes, I am quite sure I have never heard of you before. And are you sure your name isn't due to the fact that you are covered in stars? You see, I thought the name was because of your rather interesting attire. You do realize you are covered in colourful stars, don't you?"

"He does have a point you know Star Bear. I had never heard of you before discovering you as my alternate pillow AND you ARE all covered in stars," said the cat.

"Yes, yes, I am very certain that I am quite the most famous bear ever. These colourful stars you see are just to emphasize how very famous I truly am. Surely, when you were on your holiday you must of heard of me as you travelled around!" stated Star Bear.

"Hmmm. I really don't think that I did. I only ever heard of you when I got back here and Fuzzy Beast had found you in Peter's room."

"Well, you must have gone to the wrong sorts of places."

"We went to lots of places. We went snorkelling at the Whitsunday Islands. We saw loggerhead turtles at Mon Repos. We went to the rainforest at Mt. Tamborine and to Dreamworld on the Gold Coast. Then there were all the other things to do and see that we COULDN'T quite squeeze in to the time we had. There was Currumbin Wildlife Sanctuary, and lots of awesome beaches, and there was even a Movie World," replied PJ.

"Well. There you have it. THAT explains everything."

"What does?" asked PJ, suddenly feeling very confused.

"Well, you DIDN'T go to Movie World, and THAT, of course, is where I would be MOST famous," said Star Bear with confidence.

"Why, are you in the movies?" asked the cat.

"I think I must be with a name like Star Bear. Right up there with Superman. It all sounds the same, don't you think? You know... Star...and Super..." asked Star Bear.

PJ and the cat looked at each other, shrugged their shoulders, and shook their heads. The cat replied with, "Hmmm. What I think is that it is YOUR turn to be a pillow!" And with that he plonked his mass of white fur down on the bear.

"Hmmm. Hmmm, hmmm hmmm hmmm," said the bear.

"Yes. My point exactly," said the cat. "Much more peaceful. Definitely time for a cat-nap!" And so, PJ and Fuzzy curled up for a snooze.

The End...

(until the next adventure!)

PJ's adventure in Queensland!

Northern Territory

Western Australia

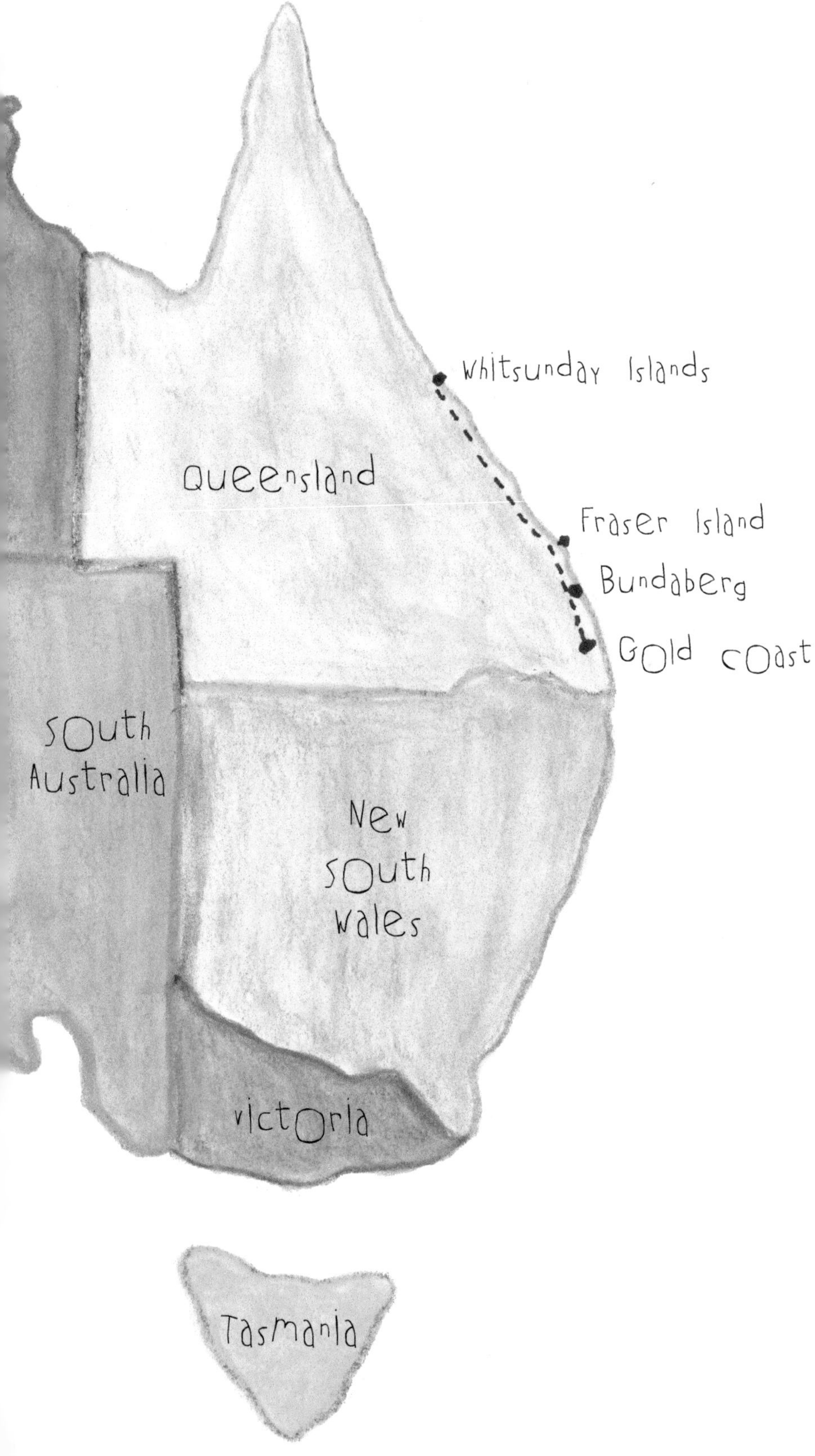

Whitsunday Islands

Queensland

Fraser Island

Bundaberg

Gold Coast

South
Australia

New
South
Wales

Victoria

Tasmania

The Travel Adventures of PJ Mouse

The Travel Adventures of PJ Mouse in Canada

PJ Mouse is going across Canada on his first adventure with his new family. Join PJ as he discovers the vastness and diversity of Canada—from glaciers, to salt lakes, to the ocean floor.

The Travel Adventures of PJ Mouse in a Small Corner of England

Join PJ and his new pal Star Bear on this, his third adventure, in jolly olde England. Discover why things like bike rides and car trips are a little too entertaining in this ancient island home.

The Travel Adventures of PJ Mouse in New Zealand

Come join PJ on this, his fourth adventure, in New Zealand. PJ discovers that New Zealand is full of wild and exciting places… sometimes a little too exciting for a timid mouse such as himself.

ABOUT THE AUTHOR
& ILLUSTRATOR

GWYNETH JANE PAGE (Jane), who holds an MBA from Simon Fraser University, has called many countries home. She and her family now reside on the Gold Coast in Queensland, Australia. The PJ Mouse stories are based on Jane's family trips with the real stuffed animal, PJ, who was found by Emily, Jane's youngest daughter.

MEGAN ELIZABETH, Jane's second oldest daughter, has been artistic since she was a little girl. Illustrating these books has enabled her to combine her love of travel with her love of art.

Gwyneth Jane Page and Megan Elizabeth's other books in this series include *The Travel Adventures of PJ Mouse — In Queensland, The Travel Adventures of PJ Mouse — In a Small Corner of England*, and *The Travel Adventures of PJ Mouse — In New Zealand*.

Printed in Australia
AUOW01n1718090818
301253AU00002B/2